TIMOTHY'S TALE

Something strange and stripy has
invaded Sergeant Major's garden,
but what is it . . .?

the Shoe People™

TIMOTHY'S TALE

It was a quiet afternoon in Shoe Town. The residents of Shoe Street were at peace with the world. Margot, the beautiful ballerina was practising the pas de deux from *Swan Lake*. Trampy was watching a flower grow and Charlie the clown was reading the *Big Top Weekly*.

Then suddenly, the serenity was
shattered by a severe shout . . . "TRAMPY!
WHAT IS THIS 'THING' DOING IN MY
GARDEN?"
    It was Sergeant Major, bellowing as
usual, and he was very angry.

Trampy sighed. What now? he thought. He stopped watching the flower growing and walked over to the fence that divided his and Sergeant Major's garden. "Don't grow too quickly while I'm away," he said to the flower. The flower nodded gently in the breeze.

"What is it, Sergeant Major?" asked Trampy. "Have some of my wild flowers grown over your fence again?"

Sergeant Major was inspecting something very closely further along the fence and didn't answer, so Trampy climbed over the fence and went to see what he was looking at.

Lying on the ground was a rope-like object with alternate black and orange bands around it. Only one end could be seen. The other end disappeared under the fence.

"THIS IS SOMETHING OF YOURS, ISN'T IT?" bellowed Sergeant Major. "ANOTHER ONE OF YOUR PLANTS THAT DOESN'T KNOW HOW TO BEHAVE PROPERLY! WELL I AM GOING TO PUSH IT BACK WHERE IT BELONGS." With that he took hold of it and started to push it back through the fence.

There was a loud roaring noise and the rope-like object started to wave around angrily. Sergeant Major leapt backwards into Trampy's arms. "HELP, SAVE ME!" he shouted. "IT'S ALIVE!"

Margot, who had heard all the shouting, came rushing along the street from Swan Lake Cottage to see what was going on. "Stand back, Margot," warned Trampy. "It seems that we have discovered a strange, stripy snake in Sergeant Major's flower bed."

"I will call P.C. Boot immediately," said Margot, and she went rushing off to Drill Hall to call the police station. She picked up the phone and dialled 999.

"Is that P.C. Boot?" she asked.

A low muttering came from the receiver.

"No," she said with exasperation, "you don't have to look in your notebook to find out who you are. I can tell it's you from your voice. Please come to Drill Hall straight away."

In a matter of moments P.C. Boot appeared on the scene. He pulled out his notebook, opened it, held his pencil poised, and finally said, "Now then, what is all this about?"

"IT'S A SNAKE!" shouted Margot, Trampy and Sergeant Major all at once. P.C. Boot started writing in his notebook. 'It has been alleged,' he wrote, 'by certain citizens, that a snake has . . .' He got no further.

"STOP FIDDLING ABOUT!" shouted
Sergeant Major. "THE SNAKE WILL DIE
OF OLD AGE WHILE YOU ARE WRITING
THINGS DOWN. WHAT I WANT TO
KNOW IS HOW AM I GOING TO GET IT
OUT OF MY GARDEN?"

P.C. Boot put his notebook back into his pocket. "All right," he said, "show me the snake." He was led to where the black and orange banded creature was still waving around angrily. The brave policeman bent down and inspected it closely.

"Hmm," he said. "That is very strange. This is the first time that I have ever seen a snake wearing a fur coat!" He prodded the snake gently with his pencil. The snake gave an enormous ROAR and started to wave round in a most threatening manner.

Trampy had a very puzzled look on his
face. "What is the matter, Trampy?" asked
Margot.

"There is no such thing in the world,"
replied Trampy, "as a roaring snake that
wears a fur coat. I suspect that we have
made a mistake in our identification. We
must call in an expert!"

"DON'T BE SILLY," said Sergeant Major. "THERE IS NO EXPERT ON HAIRY SNAKES IN SHOE TOWN!"

"Oh yes there is!" said a voice from behind them. They all turned. It was Charlie the clown.

"I am an expert on strange and mysterious animals from all over the world," said Charlie.

"PAH!" snorted Sergeant Major in disbelief. "WHAT WOULD A STUPID CLOWN KNOW?"

"Show me your hairy snake and I will tell you," said Charlie.

They took him to the scene of the snake.

Charlie took a quick look at the hairy snake and said, "That is no snake. That . . . is a tiger!"

"A TIGER?" sneered Sergeant Major. "TIGERS AREN'T LONG AND THIN, TIGERS ARE BIG . . . WITH GREEN EYES . . . AND TEETH."

"Like that?" asked Charlie, pointing to
the top of the fence. Sergeant Major's eyes
popped out as a tiger's head appeared
over the top of the fence at the same time
as the tiger's tail, the hairy snake,
disappeared under the bottom.

At the sight of such a huge and hairy beast, there was much consternation and confusion among the assembled group. P.C. Boot whipped out his notebook and started scribbling furiously, Margot did fourteen pirouettes without stopping and Sergeant Major stood to attention and saluted repeatedly.

Only Trampy and Charlie were not
affected by the tiger. "All right," said
Trampy. "Calm down." The others
stopped scribbling, spinning, and saluting.
"Now," said Trampy, turning to Charlie the
clown. "What are we going to do about
the tiger?"

"The tiger is quite tame," said Charlie.
"See, here in the *Big Top Weekly* . . ." he
held out the newspaper, "it says 'LOST,
TIMOTHY THE TIMID TIGER. LIKES
OVERGROWN GARDENS AND FAIRY
CAKES. IF FOUND, PLEASE RING THE
CIRCUS.'"

Before Timothy went back to the circus, they all had a tea party at Margot's house, with plenty of fairy cakes. Everybody had two each except for Margot, who was very ladylike and only had one, and Timothy, who was very tigerlike and had one hundred and forty-six.